Ziggy Marley

One day I was in my kitchen making breakfast with my then three-year-old daughter Judah. She looked at me and said, "I love you." I spontaneously replied to her, "I love you too." From that came the song and now the book based on the lyrics. I hope you share and enjoy this with your loved ones as I have with mine.

I love you too.

Ziggy

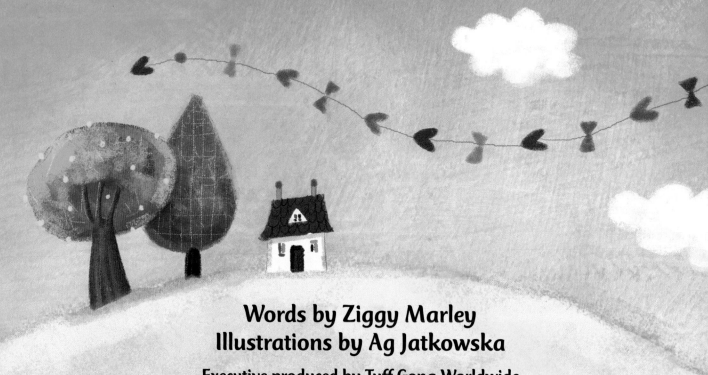

Words by Ziggy Marley
Illustrations by Ag Jatkowska

Executive produced by Tuff Gong Worldwide

© 2014 Tuff Gong Worldwide, LLC
℗ "I Love You Too" lyrics published by Ishti Music, Inc.

Published by Akashic Books/Tuff Gong Worldwide Books

ISBN-13: 978-1-61775-310-7
First printing

Akashic Books | PO Box 1456 | New York, NY 10009
info@akashicbooks.com | www.akashicbooks.com

Thank you to my mother Rita, my
sister Cedella, and my daughter Judah.

I Love You Too is dedicated to all the children of the world. I love you.
—Ziggy

I love you too, I love you too.
I tell you, I love you.

I love you too, I love you too.
I love you.

When you smile, I'll smile along.

When you cry, my comfort comes.

When you walk, I'll be beside you,
holding your hands.

When the sun comes out, we play.
I'll never be far away.

When you tell me that you love me,
this is what I'm gonna say...

I love you too,
I love you too.
I tell you,
I love you.

I love you too, I love you too.
I love you.

Like the fish loves the sea.

Like the honey and the bee.

Like a lizard loves to climb,
up into a tree.

Like a bird loves to fly,
way up in the sky.

Like a worm loves to go, way down low.

I love you too, I love you too.
I tell you, I love you.

I love you too, I love you too. I love you.

Like the grass loves to be green...
and the earth loves to be clean.

Like the sun loves to shine...

and the monkey loves to climb.
Hey, it happens naturally.

And that's the way it's got to be.
And the worm still loves to go,
way down low.

I love you too, I love you too.
I tell you, I love you.

I love you too, I love you too.
I love you.

From the first time that I saw you,
I knew that it was true.

There will be a lifelong time to spend.
Around the corner, around the bend.
Up the hills and through the valleys.

No matter how things change,
this one thing will remain.
I'll sing it again and again...

I love you too, I love you too.
I tell you, I love you.
I love you too, I love you too.
I love you.

I love you too, I love you too.
I tell you, I love you.
I love you too, I love you too.

I love you too, I love you too.
I tell you, I love you.
I love you too, I love you too.

I love you too, I love you too. I tell you, I love you.

YOU

UNLIMITED RESOURCES
GIVING ENLIGHTENMENT
(U.R.G.E.)

is a charitable organization founded by
ZIGGY MARLEY

U.R.G.E. seeks to make enduring contributions to the lives of children in Jamaica, Africa, and throughout the world. U.R.G.E. acts to support education, health, and the environment, in efforts to improve the communities where children live and grow, as they are our future's unlimited resource. The more we can give to them, the more enlightened we can become.

U.R.G.E.
UNLIMITED RESOURCES GIVING ENLIGHTENMENT

www.urgefoundation.org

U.R.G.E. MISSION

ACTION

· Seek communities that may benefit from our help.

· Raise funds via individual and corporate donations, product sales, ticket sales, and charitable events.

· Collect and donate the items (clothing, toys, school supplies, food) that are most needed by children and their communities.

· Provide assistance and resources that enable communities to develop and self-sustain.

AWARENESS

· Raise awareness on current events, social developments, and political landscapes which affect children.

· Partner with other artists, celebrities, brands, and charitable organizations to draw attention to the needs of the communities in need of donations.

· Research the most accurate and unbiased information to the media and the public.

· Share our stories of success through photos, stories, and letters.

ZIGGY MARLEY is a devoted father and husband, a multiple Grammy Award winner, an Emmy Award winner (for his song "I Love You Too" in the animated series *3rd & Bird*), humanitarian, singer, songwriter, producer, and reggae icon, who has released fifteen critically acclaimed albums. His early immersion in music came at age ten when he sat in on recording sessions with his father, Bob Marley. As the front man of Ziggy Marley and the Melody Makers, he released eight best-selling albums, with such chart-topping hits as "Look Who's Dancing," "Tomorrow People," and "Tumblin' Down." Ziggy's first solo album, *Dragonfly*, was released in 2003 and was followed by two Grammy Award–winning solo albums, *Love Is My Religion* (Best Reggae Album) and *Family Time* (Best Children's Album).